Sunhats And Raincoats

©Alys Maia

All rights reserved

The right of Alys Maia to be identified
As author of this work has been asserted by her
In accordance with the
Copyright, Design and Patents Act, 1988.

Alys Maia

Email:alys511@ymail.com

All rights reserved

No part of this publication may be reproduced, stored in a retrieval
System, or transmitted in any form or by any means, electronic,
Mechanical, photocopying, recording or otherwise, without
The prior permission of the author.

Introduction

Why did I decide to gather a collection
of thematic poetry?

It has always occurred to me
that each month reminds me of something
or someone.
Various experiences, objects, situations
and people in general.
And this all seems to happen in a powerful way,
via my dreams, the weather, things I've seen and heard
or emotions that I've felt
And so with twelve months... one year... that repeat themselves year in year out,
It could be likely, that we could take each month for granted
As they continuously fall into and out of each other,
like we fall in and/ or out of love
We may sail through some months, while others,
could be an absolute struggle

And so, in September 2020,
I wrote my first 'proper' poem while gazing
onto a peaceful early evening sky.
This first poem
is the beginning of my choice of creative thoughts
and is under the title of *My September*

Dedication:

This book is dedicated to beautiful friends
who have always taken the time to read my work.
In particular, Annie and Ralph.
And also to Andrew Brown, who's poetry
has enabled me to find alternative ideas of my own
I'm eternally grateful to everyone for their support

Contents:

September.....Pages 13 – 17
My September.....14
Sharing.....15
Finding Me.....16
Star Calling.....17

March.....Pages 19 – 23
Painted Paper.....20
The Greeting.....21
Vernal Equinox.....22
When March Arrived.....23

July.....Pages 25 - 29
Thoughts Of July.....26
Whistle Down The River.....27
Orange Is Not The Only Colour.....28
Feeling Good.....29

February.....Pages – 31 - 35
You Are.....32
The Knot Maker.....33
The Silver Lining.....34
The Feb Flower.....35

October.....Pages 37 - 41
On The Solstice.....38
Slow Moments.....39
The Weather Veil.....40
October Youth.....41

May.....Pages 43 - 47
The Field Trip.....44
Nocturnal Desire.....45
All In One Day.....46
Sea Spell.....47

The Haze Of The Moon.....Pages 49 - 57
The Calm.....50
Dewdrop Tears.....51
On The Horizon.....52
The Edge Of The Water.....53
Within A Moon.....54
Sadness.....55
The Plight.....56
Like The Moon.....57

Contents continued:

January.....Pages 59 - 63
The Phase.....60
Between The Branches.....61
Love In Flight.....62
Dreamworld.....63

November.....Pages 65 - 69
The Dance In The Lane.....66
The Giant.....67
November City.....68
Doorways And Pathways.....69

August.....Pages 71 - 75
Melodies.....72
Kernow Light.....73
Hey Daisy.....74
Nature Travels.....75

December.....Pages 77 - 81
The Solstice.....78
Swapping Places.....79
The Clouds.....80
The Contours Of December.....81

April.....Pages 83 - 87
But For The Fools.....84
The Need To Get Out More.....85
April Comfort.....86
Blossom Road.....87

June.....Pages 89 - 93
Fragments.....90
Sun Catching.....91
June For Love.....92
Before The Storm.....93

The Whirlwind.....Pages 95 – 103
Where Has It All Gone.....97
What The Months Mean To Me.....99
In A Whirlwind.....101
Lovers.....103

September

My September

September whispering
to an introvert's dream...
The sadness of summer...
An uncertain winter...
And always, the in-between.

September whispering to the sun as it falls
While fading away as another month calls.
It sees every summer
And each winter it sighs...
to the nip in the air;
Another month in disguise.

But you will always be here
September asleep.
A month we so loved, but just couldn't keep.

And what now have,
is our talking with passion...

To the artist and author

The poet, the singer

The entwined lovers...

And the sadness...
of summer.

So as we move closer to winter
unseen,
we remain in September...
Our month
in-between
Entwine as two lovers
Like an introverts dream.

Sharing

I spoke to the flowers but they were asleep
I have spoken while they were awake?
I told them the secret that you couldn't keep
I had to pour it out somehow
Maybe they heard me, weary and bleak
Maybe they heard nothing at all
Maybe I told them a story too deep
So I wait for the petals to wake
And do my best to be there should they weep

Finding Me

Early morning under a hollow sun
I have the need to rest
I am not complete, but I am one
And that is my success

Misty dawn, opaque sun
I don't want to be out there
Your image of a day begun
is spreading here and there

I'm sorry, I am done today
But you have work ahead, I see
Hollow sun, be filled with light
And in your haven I will be

Middle morning, tidal views
awaken me each day
I may be done, and slightly weary,
but I still plan to cast away

Finding me will not be easy
There is a secret place
I shall smile in lazy dreaming
And I shall contemplate

Star Calling

The passion you have
A star that keeps twisting
twisting and turning with love
Crystal the night
Warm and precise
Defined
and so wordly
And known to be wise

The Star from the wild
Calling it's fans,
to step right inside and explore

Weave your way through
the star and it's sounds
And don't forget the depth
of the view

March

Painted Paper

It was a Painted Lady Butterfly, and it was made entirely from paper.
Thin and finely etched upon,
As thin as biscuit wafers.
It was torn, I saw the flaw upon its wing,
wings, so perfect and so thin.

It was a Painted Lady Butterfly, and you, were it's creator.
You made it from the finest aged and crinkled paper.
It only flew when days were still
For it knew it would be safer.

And how it came to life this way,
I may never come to know.
I thought she'd only take her flight,
if breezes let her go.

So the enchanted,
Painted Butterfly,
floated in your view.
By chance, she flew onto my hair,
but her magic came,
from you.

The Greeting

You are the Roman god of war
You will warmly greet the sun
And with charm, you come,
and you explore
But always in your peaceful war

You work by day and night
You will be the one to soar...
And help the lower sun
to rise...
For the new can now
explore
...And tiptoe through the undergrowth,
where the sacred warrior sleeps
And grazing next to shallow pools
that listen as we speak

The Roman god of war and peace,
brings nature to the shore
And to the gentle rain
that falls...
For the calm before the storm

The Vernal Equinox

I was there in the sky
One minute... floating
The other... just high.
I remember the parlour,
and the vanilla ice-cream

I think it was the equinox,
that brought me this dream

It came to us smiling
And we stood on the pier
Put on our sunhats
Spring is now here.
More rain tomorrow
With a sun heading north
But who paid for the ice-cream
that the equinox bought?

I think it was Mada
She came with the rain
With sunhats and raincoats
And hope, yet again

When March Arrived

She is the violin, she knows a fellow cello

Musically...
she's merciful
Mysteriously...
he's mellow

She hits a note, caresses the strings
Moves the bow... the branches swing
She'll take the fore, let music pour...

She's everything this spring

He comes to join the violin,
and they inspire so much rain.
It pours from music in the clouds...

They are the sunlight and sunray

Ambition, passion...
And always mellow
The Cello is the one...
The one to wake her, and find her bow
And now they work as one

Merciful, she is a saviour, and a long forgotten face
The mellow fellow is by her side,
and their hearts begin to race

Fetch the canoe! Spring is here
Walking shoes and bottled beer
See the bow and hear it move
A violin in spring, for you!

Flowers anchor as leaves will green
Push out your boat, and buy vanilla ice cream
Hope for the sunlight
Dance for its rays
Forget the canoe! It's seen better days

July

Thoughts Of July

I'm wandering into the months ahead,
and as always, I'm wondering why.

Today I'm talking
and I'm clearly sharing my thoughts
with the summer, July.

A night of heat...
my mind moving quickly
at too fast a pace...like July
But I told you I'd look to the months that follow
Although this month has not said goodbye.

A night plays a chorus
And the shrill for the air
is adorning the buzz of July.
Maybe I long for...
the time that we have here
Maybe this is the reason why...

I want to hold on to everyone...
and everything I've longed for...

Hold onto the rest of July

But we must let her leave,
For we'll see her next year
As she, is like time
and will fly.

Whistle Down The River

Playing a tin whistle
Picking apples from the trees,
you line the riverbank with music,
while down on both your knees.

Bearing your entire soul,
to the time you fell in love
You play the music as you weep
And you think of those above.

You wonder if they see you,
now that you are free
Then gather all the apples picked,
and get up from your knees.

Strolling to my cottage
with a feather on your cap
A whistle in your canvas bag
And a flower for my hat.

Orange Is Not The Only Colour

An orange line has taken the sky
but soon, it will be fading away
Watch it leaving the familiar horizon...
the panoramic

slipping

and sliding,

into the dystopian view of today

And to be replaced, by bloodshot red
and obscure cryptic lines
Again... again,
keep on looking,
at the entirety of the sky

Sunset surfing over waves...
Behind the houses,
the sky ablaze
Slipping lines, that slide away
into the night...
the hiding place

Behold, behold
Like a shawl...
of deepest red, behind the wall...
this sky has drawn a mountain range
The french-like alps, that time will change

And orange is not the only line
To flood lamp an entire sky

Feeling Good

I take the flowers from inside my boots
I'm good, and couldn't give two hoots
Now shall we sit beside the moat where coots will swim the day away

A friend, she gave me useful tips
So I found a way to paint my lips
Then precariously ate the chunky chips
What a lovely day

I'm far too tired to even think
Maybe I could do with forty winks
Just like the owl that hoots,
and beats the day away
But like the lifestyle of the coot
I just seem to go astray

February

You Are

Like flakes of coconut, you delicately fall
Like flour being sifted, you float
You decorate the roses, tucked up so small
You look so attractive
tonight.

You are dressed in a gown for an evening ball
You are glitter on the petals you coat
With vibrance you stand in the old stately hall
You really are
a beautiful sight.

The palest of velvet
A bed for the snow
Nothing will move them,
and he wants you to know...
That nothing
can move him as much as you do.
As you float like those petals
Ohhh the beautiful
you.

The Knot Maker.

His boat has taken a beating
from the strength of the good outdoors
So he's training ropes,
around his boat
Another winter away
from the shore.

His boat, his pride, his only love,
touches the harbour rise
He knows so much
About so many knots
and the colours he paints them,
will capture the eye.

His life has taken a beating
from the strength of the life he knew
So he's busy caring for the sea that calls
And the ropes he trails,
along harbour walls
The knots he ties
that tear his hands
The cold and blustery weather that stands…
For winter and worn out boats
And calls for scraves
and padded coats.

His boat, his joy, and he himself,
make this town…
just something else

The Silver Lining

There is a cloud that sees your sorrow smiling,
and a laugh that lingers on
I shan't ignore that silver lining,
or your humour that I need

The ins and outs of all that smiling,
and the guess work that we do
The slowly sinking
uphill climbing
My memories of you...
that shine inside the silver lining
of the clouds, up there
in view

February Flower

You tell me I should tie my lace
But I'm wiping tears from my face
You pick a flower
I bend the stem, while playing with my unstitched hem

I need to see this winter go
It's January now and she must know
That we are waiting,
and long to see, those other flowers, released from seeds

And brightness will surely be
a theme
So we keep on going...

Dare to dream

Let us walk, I'll wipe my face
And I think I'd better tie my lace

October

On The Solstice

Show us the working of your soul
The authentic you, that we've all yet to know
The mortality and passion
The tenderest touch
And the pleasure of summer
We need it that much.

The new fluent words,
spoken from the mind
A sacred song, we rarely can find
But they are here for the summer
with the height of the stars
A solstice that wonders...
Just who you are

Slow Moments

A shorter month,
That will soon be over
Not in days,
but in moments
When the weeks got colder
as they gathered my grief.
So...
many...
moments...
of disbelief.

October
Painting a picture of the leaves
With a need for hope
being carved onto trees.

Weighed down heavily
Is an empty loss
Like the leaves
That fall on you
With a camouflage touch

A treetop surrounded
by a mass of colour
A sun filled day
with a stem for every flower.
All may be lost, but still will be yours
October
I need you to slow down
and pause

The Weather Veil

A smoldering fire, losing it's flare and it's flames
A bedraggled sky, with the oncoming rain.
The dancing, spiraling, falling
of rust,
that departs from the trees
and gathers like dust

Gather together, part of a trail
The mist with it's cloak,
like a wedding dress veil
The wilting and ghosting of
dampening air...
It keeps returning to us
with no cross to bear

We notice you more, tune into your tone
And wait here for something,
And we are often alone
You're a beauty to some
But many will dread
the lowering mist
above the brown, the red...
The bedraggled sky
draped like a veil
And the dying of life
on the gathering trail

October Youth

Being in Rhoose airport
on a Sunday afternoon
Where planes that leave the runway,
will be heading for the moon.

Aber Halt on Saturday
I'm waiting for a train
Should have found another station
as the wind up here's insane.

Jacobs market, any day!
A pocket watch on show
Antique jewellery, old LP's
Books and quirky clothes.

I walked an unkempt pathway,
many many times
Often I was there alone
with a head and heart of rhymes.

But then I had no thoughts of markets...
Or all those trips I took for granted
Pathways, books and old LP's
So I'm now recalling memories...

while I can

May

The Field Trip

I'd like the flow of life to meander
like that river at Oxwich Bay
To gather my thoughts,
catch up with the pace...
and chill

I'd like to see the meander again
And the heron, a delicate grey
I'd like to gather my thoughts,
and for now, just lock 'em away...
and chill

I wouldn't mind seeing those photos again
The feeling of being sixteen
The day I learned of the works
of the river,
which 'til then,
had been a meandering dream

Nocturnal Desire

The forecast says we'll have rain overnight
I relish it's perfection,
and have a nocturnal desire to be truly awoken
To be awake overnight, and asleep for the day;
Hearing and feeling the rain at play

Like the thinkers who think and the writers that write,
I want to tap into it all

With rain on the way and in sinc with a song,
Be creative and endlessly let it pour, let it fall
Jump a puddle in the dark
But I'm not sure I can
For I'm not a sleeper by day

All In One Day

Maia holds her head up to the light,
"twenty three days"
she whispers to me
"I'm counting the weeks
'til the summer"

Maia is confident,
and he knows what to say
She's like the spring and the summer,
all in on day.

Positive is she,
with her head to the light
Are are trusting her now?
Has she got it right?

Let's follow Maia,
the happiest one
Who knew it was spring
before it had even begun.

Twenty three days
for his twenty years
He arrived in the spring,

and *he* will always be here.

Sea Spell

It gives it's everything,
throws itself to the cliffs.
Alters it's pace,
exhales and rebounds
Then turns back
to the space,

of the sea.

One wave, take me kindly
And wrap me up well
In safety,
I would find thee...
And deep in the spell...

we could dwell,
we could dwell,

by the sea.

One wave is folding, as it's urging me so
And I imagine myself, adrift as we go...
And untouched we would be
In the warmth of the waves,

as we breathe,
as we breathe,

with the sea.

For the cliffs and the souls,
we rebound,
we let go...
We give all or nothing
to the cliffs and the foam...

of the waves, of the waves.

And the choices we've made
And the love that we have,

For the sea

The Haze Of The Moon

The Calm

Breathe away...
the feeling will pass...
These emotions always do
And you will still be here,
watching light,

as it drips,

as it drips

from the moon

Breathe away
always...to the beat
of your own heart
Focus on the moon,
such a gracious curve of art

Breathe, then listen
to the dripping
of the oils,
working on the touches...
The moon will hear your voice

Speak, in all your solitude
And the moon will breathe away...

before she fades
into her own light

And before she comes
to us again

Dewdrop Tears

I see tears falling from the moon
And they are perfectly formed,
like the dew

All that they weep for, is here as we speak
And all that they weep for,
is here as we seek

...For answers to questions
That beauty we found,
now fractured and lost
But what goes around...

Will come back as a dewdrop
full-circle it turns
To find all that it cares for,
is still lost in the world

All that it weeps for
will turn, then decay
And all we can do,
is find other ways

On The Horizon

She rose over the river and settled on the horizon
of blue.
Touched the water,
as if her soul
was in sight...
and touching you.

And not a breeze in the air
not a chill, nor a care;
Just her on the water
on the deep midnight blue.

She sits in her own light,
she is larger than life.
Colours the water, from the left...
to the right.
With profoundness, and detail
she embraces the sky
Not a chill, nor a care...
not tonight, and we know why...

She has found, and sits above,
a yellow sailing boat.
She's observing all the hours,
while keeping us afloat.
She is wisdom in the making
Knows when to fade,
and when to leave.
But for now, she will sit upon
the abundance of the sea.

Her golden face, her tender smile
We are her image of the night
Her mind at rest, within our hearts...

She fades away...

and out of sight...

The Edge Of The Water

Sailing on the ocean, over the reflection of the night
Where a crescent band of is waiting, to be your faithful guide.

A hand-made wooden sailing boat, sees a man-made golden moon.
It looks white,
against the sea I sail on,
as I am on my way to you

Across the ocean, gallant lives
have been looking for the new
And if they were here with me tonight,
they would have found that
from the moon

It travels onwards
and underneath,
the bouyant sailing boat
Upon the waves I sail away
just with the moon, afloat

Meet me on the waters edge,
for I am on my way to you
Your gallant life intrigues me so
Somehow, you made it through

Jagged driftwood awaits in red
Torn between the waters edge
It grazes pebbles
And sings farewell
to stories cupped into the shell

Within A Moon

A moon within a moon
I see a prism in the blue
And a hint of light upon my eyes...
is the earth,
you left,
too soon.

I have come this far to find you
and I decide to stand alone
Then follow the wind that brought me here,
until I come across your home

A moon within another moon
I'll be heading that way soon
Where darkness hangs,
so undisturbed,
and the prism turns to blue

For I have come this way,
this far...
to see the moon in front of me
But I hear the words
from me to you...
But they can't bring you...
to me

Sadness

You're a ladder away from the troublesome moon
Weary and pale,
it is waiting for you
It has seen today's sadness,
as it rose from the sky
Then it lost all the will
to glow on this night

But you know the moon
like the back of your hand
You study in awe, and then... watch it stand,
between all of those rocks,
and between all the lives,
of another day lost,
under a darkening sky

You bond with the crescent,
and you cry as it fades...
deep into the dark sky...
where the river cascades
If you could only stand higher,
reach out, or step up...
You'd see a colour of life
that's about to erupt...

The boldness of night
that clings to it's love
And this moon you are watching,
is brightening up
Bold is the moon
as you urge it to glow...
from the depth of your wishes
And from the will of your hopes

The Plight

The moon in full,
gravitational pull
The mirror shines tonight
No better way, to sleep 'til dawn
than to hand the moon, your plight

The frozen moon
It's far too soon
to know when life could thaw
Far too cold to touch our hearts
It's far too late for sure

The mirror speaks,
a full cartoon
The outlined shapes and form
A sober sketch
A freezing circle
that somehow keeps us warm

The moon in full,
gravitational pull
The mirror gleams tonight
See it thaw, then turn full circle
Farewell to every plight

Like The Moon

You are like the moon,
divine and unique
A soul and a dreamer
A true masterpiece

You are sat beside me,
in a deep sombre mood
The ambiance above us
shedding light, as it moves

You've invited the darkness
into this room
And I don't imagine you leaving,
anytime soon

Now is the moment
where I feel I can dream
The moon, may it guide you,
so much closer to me

We sit amongst shadows
in the contours of light
The moon feels the kiss
as we bring on the night

How rich the encounter
How sacred the moon
It's a soul, and a dreamer
And so unique,
as are you

January

The Phase

January saw the past as a chilly winter tour

But looked for something different
and wanted something more

He started looking onwards
to a further changing phase

Where older thoughts would escape his mind,
in search for brighter days.

He had a party
There was no one there
Just him and Peter Pan
A blanket on the sofa
And another Facebook ban.

He had a crush on Wendy
He thought it was a phase
But Wendy saw her life on tour
And flew right off the page

With every breeze...
Someone somewhere
will notice Peter Pan
He flies the skies
of January

He's the only one who can

Between The Branches

Lines like veins flowing down, and trickle onto unpredictable ground
Flickering lamps
and the dimming of light
With the veins of the ice branching out to the night.
    Veins changing colour
      as they dilute on the way...
      to the static painted trees, for a shimmering display.
Icy, icy and opaque the lamp.
A slippery surface for a shimmering dance
Veins unbreakable, colours that seize
All under a moonlight
that seeps between trees.
      Gleam on and sparkle, this ice upon ground
      Uniquely it loves, what winter has found!
Ice upon branches
Ice cold for the streets
Winter portraying it's life
with a freeze
Detailed the shadows,
Intricately bold
Another moment of a life...
on hold.
      Branches that shimmer, under the strength of the moon
      And the lightness of snow...
      where nothing could bloom.
But we are warmed by the glow, like the branches that touch
And we hear them all crackle
They can deal with so much
      Moon, will you shine between many a branch
      Where the frost will keep biting, at every chance.
We turn towards winter and hear every sound...
from the sharpness of ice
as it captures the ground.

And close to our hearts...
is the winter that frowns.

Love In Flight

Sapphire wings, smoothness of silk
And veins in both hands,
absorbing dew on his palms
A lovers name, carved onto stone
And the words...
I am lost without you

Oh to rise through the air,
with the dew on her hair
And to search for the love
found by *he*

The sapphire soul
being the name on the stone
And that beautiful soul,
being *she*

In the palms of his hands, were the lines and the forms
Of what he had been lies in amongst any truth

But all he could think of was the sapphire soul

And the words *I am lost without you...*

Dream World

Love me,
Love me not
But I will always be under the sunspot
Catching my dreams, before they escape
And as it so happens,
I'm lucky today

I have the breeze on my side
And captured a dream,
I'm not sure it's mine,
but it makes sense to me

As green as the patchwork,
and the roots,
and the stem
As blue as the dye,
and the buds, where you dwell...
I have lived in my dream world since the start of my life
And under the sunspot,
with a love by my side

Love me, or not,
Your sincerity, it shows
For I have been in your warmth,
 where the winter sun glows

And so,
We stood by the Birch,
Heard the silence the church
We didn't pray,
didn't see where we'd been

We gathered our senses,
on the patchwork of green
...that's how we met and I captured your dream

November

The Dance In The Lane

An evening breeze, reaching out to the leaves,
as they lie undisturbed in the lane
A gentle swaying is coming this way
And the leaves, they respond
and obey.
The stirring breeze is gaining it's strength,
Picking up pace
and finding its space...
A singular leaf wakes to a dance
Ahh, the breeze is calling... and more take a chance
A group of them rise
See the dance come to life
They chatter and sing as they sway to the music
that once lay asleep under trees
They continue to gather
Ahh see the flight...
of these turbulent leaves under the dimmest light.
The breeze it will whisper
And the winds, they will sigh...
as more leaves are chanting, and lifted up high
Twisting in pairs,
they talk to the night
Holding each other
like dancers on ice.
Ahh, see them glide in the dark of the lane
The only light from themselves,
on display.
Rustic the dress and the dance so precise
Capture a moment you'll never see twice.
More leaves gather and rise in the air
Turning and landing on my windy-blown hair
A dance of a lifetime
All thanks to the trees
Nature's performance,
is as wild as can be.

The Giant

Autumn wound, electric blue
The calm before the storm
Starstruck lovers, in the sky,
that haven't yet been born

A simple sky, it dazzles life,
as a giant dressed in blue
He walks into, the sunny shadows
I see the crimson hue

Tie-dye patterns, works of art
The storm that never came
Beside the garden gate you stand,
under a sky becoming lame

Autumn wound, call on me,
and tell me what they saw...
beside the blue and giant cloud,
that never formed a storm

November City

We are restless like the Sea
I am there, somewhere with you
And you are somewhere,
here,
with me

We are reckless like the waves,
as they await the weather change
The coastal pathway, almost clear
as clear as our ways

We are simply reckless beings
somewhere down the line
But cold, and in its silent tempo,
the waves have formed a line

Cities yell but this place whispers...
And when I'm out of sorts,
we come and rescue reckless people...
who fall upon the shore

Doorways And Pathways

You will walk through every doorway of your life,
with your eyes open,
an open mind,
and a heart full of hope
And you will do this,
because it's what you've always done

You have shown us every pathway, every year
And smoothly painted stones, will see you tread on them at night.

And planets we explored will be where tired eyes will hide.

And more, much more... So much hope inside.

You will walk through every doorway of your life,
For all your life for sure
With your eyes and mind in focus
And your heart, with depth, will chime
This is what you've always done
This is what you'll do

On smoothly painted stones you'll go,
You're November through and through

August

Melodies

Let your love flow into the dust
...of August

So quiet are the melodies for our memories
...Found in August

We will flow, and keep on lapping up your ways
For your music is the soul of our summer
And we'll be losing all of this some day

...August moves away

Music echoes
between the strings
and the streets
So silent are the dreams
The ones we long to keep.

Melodies making August...
And August sets us free...

It's heart and soul

It's wishes

It's clouds that travel...
silently.

It's sun and rain
And once again...
We gather August,
picture it,
place it in our view
And then we sit and talk about it
The peridot to you

Kernow Light

Late in evening on the edge of the field
Where the last rays of sunlight
are rest on my spine
I may rarely turn to look onto you
but I will always bid you
goodnight.

Summer sun, capturing the wheat in the field
like a veil unto the goodnight
I don't need to see you,
my tinted fine sun.
But I will focus on all of your light.

Evening sun, I will sit here with you
With heather bound at my feet
As I watch for your colour
watch it grow richer
watch you tint
every fine blade
of wheat.

And one more day of Cornish air...
that warmed my spine...
and coloured my hair...
now disperses it's mango light
And settles somewhere
Tonight.

Hey Daisy

Lazy daisy
Wake up, wake up

You're needed for the chain
Petal layers
close together
I'm calling you again

Petal number twenty four
Daisy daisy,
I thought there were many more,

Crazy daisy
Why not wake up?
You are needed for her hair
A friendship circle
Hugs and all
Pierced stems
Ringlets small

Upon the bride so fair

The daisy lady waits for you
You've slept for seven hours
Trail away across the fence
The forecast says "no showers"

I can make you such a garland
I can make myself a gem

Wake up, wake up
Come spread your seeds
And if not now, then when?

Well I am just the lady,
well that is a possibly, maybe
Piercing stems, the softest scent,
I'm threading time with me

Wake up, wake up
Crazy daisy
Wake up, get up and go

Nature Travels

Every breeze... An individual
Each one of them,
has significance.
Such a flow,
a flow, of speech.
Given
by the freedom
of the air.

But as nature knows
That nature kills
That nature thrives
That nature lives

And so each breeze... Is illusive still
Every one of them,
Here to spill,
to spill and give...
You,
And I,
A sense of freedom from the air.

December

The Solstice

Winter walking
Solstice spoken
Tradition talking
World awoken
Solstice
sacred
Timeless treasures
Winter
wise
As walkers tread...

Through these hours
A pagan way
On a cold, but certain
Solstice day
Winter woken
Solstice wise
We wander
with a dreamer's eyes.

Swapping Places

Well let me share my dream with you
About an autumn that followed a winter and managed to make itself known
All that we had was the barren and eiry...
until Autumn returned
for a hug.

A hug and a chat
Just like the dream
Or a glass of good whiskey
And a pizza supreme.

So winter stood waiting
for an Autumn to cover...
its wrinkled hands,
like those crinkle cut leaves...
The smiles that have aged,
but still have what it takes
And those who had left us,
could do as they please.

Those brief little bursts
Those glimmers of life
I don't think it will happen.
But in my dreams, we just might...
feel that hug.

The Clouds

All is grey,
They left,
They went away
They didn't even explain,

...or say

So we looked upwards,
and we saw them bow
With dignity they sailed away...

Then they left us in the grey

All was white
They left at night
They didn't say the time was right

...or give anything away

But we were fine,
and watched them overlap in play...

Then they left us in the grey

All was black
They shan't come back
They even took their favourite hats

...they once wore them down the bay
And I for one, recall that day

It was before they left us
...in the grey

The Contours Of December

Hills made from crepe
In the places we'd escape to if we could
But far we are from the beauty, by far
With an ancient year creeping up from afar
And we age with it all

but do we know who we are?

The contour out there,
It's smothered with hollowness
Rippling over all that is bare
Beauty, beauty,
it's just everywhere
If we can sense it, and bear up to,
the cold

A ghost by the slope.
The gradual seeping,
of the love for December and the care for the sleeping
The ones who lie out and lie under the cold
Beauty neglected,
like a sad story told.

By far, the more beautiful
are the contours of many
But if only we could see life

from afar.

April

But For The Fools

April was here
for the fools we can be
And it will leave us to be
our own fools.
Falling in love with the far reaching flowers.
And the desire to become someone new.

Oh but the chill
of the April illusion.
And the thrill of falling in love.
Open your heart
to the beginning of something.
Especially
if love's not enough.

April is waking to a difficult light.
One day so gloomy
Another so bright
Showers? Oh yes!
April has those.
And boy do we need them
Ask April she knows.

She is the wise one
And we can be fooled
By all that she shows us...
Depends on her mood.

Nesting in treetops
or on barren land.
Nature knows everything.
But us?
We need to plan.

April has woken
in search of it's life
She will come to us restless.
But put up a fight.

The Need To Get Out More

Yes I need to gather blades of grass, freshly cut or long
Barely damp, old and tough
Or even parched from the sun.

I need to step outdoors.
See the lawn, and touch the air
And if I count the paving stones,
I could end up anywhere.

I certainly do...
I need to get out...
I need to get out more.
Perhaps I'll stand out in the rain
and pray for it to pour

Then count the raindrops
one by one
Or spider webs,
just newly spun.

I need to see things from outside
Garden centres
Cars and shops
People buying seeds and pots.

But here I'm safe and occupied,
inside the great indoors
I have my mind,
so what d'ya think...
Should I really get out more?

April Comfort

The hat
The wool so pale and pretty,
so delicate and thin
I see these little threads as being the perfect thing for spring

My umbrella
As a canopy, to protect me from above
And the pitter patter
of rainfall droplets,
are truly what I love

The hat
Made from straw or linen
A bow in pale, pale peach
And if the sun comes out today,
I will wear this on the beach

Blossom Road

Apple blossom petals roll...
They curl, unfold,
at the edge of your home.

But I drive away, from blossom road.
And onto polluted, smog-ridden roads
Then onto a lane, of the motorway noise.
At the edge of the farmland,
and the good of the soil.

And I look at the pylons,
sturdy for life.
And the trees that are layered
with pollution,
but thrive.
I stay on the motorway,
I notice the sign...

Ah I remember

A4119 ----
----narrow lanes
----for two miles

Sunlight keeps dipping,
zig zag, the roads.
Light keeps appearing between
telegraph poles.

But look at the farmland, the glorious views.
And that sign on the truck says *delivered for you*

Into the slow lane,
and over cats eyes.
I loved being a kid, taken out,
on night rides.

But there is no apple blossom, found on these lanes
Just the choking of trees between pollution that preys!

June

Sun Catching

Here come the roses
with sunny patches
White pearl smoothness,
and a petal that catches...

The light

Here come the bluebells
Down where the tree fell.
On with the warm spell
enjoying what time tells...

Us all

Roses, roses, pass them around
In for a penny
A bloom for a pound.
Bluebells lying and touching the ground
Lost with the time that can never be found.

In life

The light on us all
Casting a spell
The smoothness of pearls
where the rugged tree fell.
Here comes the nature,
like partners in rhyme
Sweet roses and bluebells
And the sipping of wine...

In the shade

June For Love

What became of the month of June
And where did it go?
And what became of you...

when it left?

I had wished that June was always here, to bathe us and to loom
And in adoration I long for him,
and I hope to reach him soon

Did you leave, with the month of June?
The one that has been to loom?
If so, did you both creep out...
and step into...
the night of blue?

Did you plan to leave together?
Or on the spur of the moment maybe?
Did you go to distant lands?
And have you any photos for me?

Do you swim such pointless journeys?
Or fly such senseless ways?
Could you have a quiet word...
So that next time,
he might stay?

Before The Storm

I feel the Ocean in the air
And I think to myself... Don't let it slip away
Don't let it go unnoticed

It's warm
Why so warm,
when I hear the coming storm?

I never learned enough about the air inside the sky
Nor the Ocean in the air

But I see the moisture,
it signals to the birds
And they know... It's time to fly

We hear them flying by
Heavy, lies the sky

Under the warmest humid air
I think... I see the flare, the rumble and the call
The call from where?
Ahh somewhere...
It tells me to return to home,
Before the storm disperses
everywhere

I was smitten by the sky
And that,
I can't deny

Beautiful illusions
Delusions of the storm
The coming storm
And the Ocean starts to rise

Getting warmer, getting closer to my home
And I *feel* the Ocean,
It is breathing, as it mingles with the air

Why so warm before a storm?
And what a way to be
There was a time,
when I never cared at all

About the illusions over me

Fragments

I see the dust fall upon the feathers of a songbird,
who bellows a call.
The dust that has risen from the earth...
then returns
Then rises, to be with the coolness of air
And in the warm but weak, rays of the sun

The songbird on the ground
is adding to the sounds, of the beckoning earth,
where grubs will be found
With patience it will wait
as it listens for the safest
moment...
To rise like the dust,
and onto the tree.
Songbird silent, finding its way
through the bark of the branches..
It's easy for him...
And through the lushness and silk
of the newly formed leaves
that dress up the trees...
I see him, moving,
I hear him, flutter
And silent I stand
with the silent songbird
And with the slow coming breeze,
right above me

I may steal a few stones,
from the years that slip by
Tiny broken off fragments
under a birds lullaby
I may etch every note
on the stones of this ground
And the trembling earth
that the songbird had found

The Whirlwind

Where Has It All Gone?

The twirl that spun, has now gone.
It rose like swarm...
As you swam.

The Cloud—
It looked like a man growing old, as it moved from another,
And let go.

Rain—
It seeped into unpolished oak.
It may dry once again... bespoke!

The Sun—
It faded your map, and you lost your way, so you took one more nap...

Hail—
You prayed.

Thunder—
You played... but you were too loud for me.

Lightening—
The fork and the sheet
Some people will fall to their feet.

The whirlwind, the loss.
The panic, the love.
The happy, the sad.
The seasons we had...
All here...
For life, will go on.

What The Months Mean To Me

They are not feathers, so light they could drift.
Neither are they wrapped up for us all, like a gift.
They are unpredictable times as they flow.
And we may see them come,
We may see them go.
They are not lost forever, if they settle somewhere.
Neither are they waiting to be captured out there.
And we may not see them,
as they come,
or as they go.
And as to where they will settle...
Well I'm not sure we know

In A Whirlwind

It's five minutes to midnight
It's less dark than I thought it would be.
I chase the shadows,
watch the fellows, and hear them saying "why aren't you asleep?"

I have a wound, a midnight itch
but it's fading as I rest.
My eyes are focused
on paisley curtains,
where the shadows look their best.

It's five minutes to midnight,
I hear my bedroom door.
It needs some oil, and colour, just like the wooden floor.

I harbour thoughts for loved ones
While the fellows talk again.
Close your eyes, drift with shadows,
just count from one to ten.

Before I knew it, time had flown
I saw the clock turn five!
It's five a.m,
I see a light
Is this the break of dawn?
Am I dreaming, I'm alive?
Shadows left me, I don't know when
Did I somehow doze?
Did I count ten?
Paisley patterns dancing,
and my tired eyes, half closed.

It's five past five, my leg is sore.
By night it seems to itch far more.
I get out of bed, to see the day
But is this whirlwind here to stay?

Lovers

"I am in love" he whispers today,
as he raises his eyes to the sun
"Hear me" he says "and know me today,
for I can't gaze at this light for too long".

There's a white shape, a forming... a vertical tunnel
It touches the sky, like a cone... like a funnel.
What month are we in, for I am in awe?
The confusion of love... and what is it for?
Our lips ... they may touch,
An escape ... we will find.
For I feel for that longing, that has lit up your mind.

"I'm in love", he says,
as he whispers his call
And his thoughts, like the funnel,
echo through walls.

He shone like a verb...
A metaphorical kiss.
Tainted in sunlight.
And bathed by his wish.

"Shhh", he just whispers
"I was caught up in the winds,
but I'm safe and I'm sane...
and saw beautiful things".

Then time...
drew us closer.
As the whirlwind unseen...
became settled and kind...

For it was all...

But a dream

Biography:

I was born in South Wales in 1967.
My family background has mixed heritage, and within this,
I mostly feel that I identify with Wales (Cymru) and Italy (Italia)
I spent a lot of time, and have a lot of, wonderful childhood memories of
both the West of Wales and Cornwall (Kernow)
I'm also an artist but draw and paint very little at the moment.
I have always been a quiet person,
and more interested in natural environments
than in city life, and maybe that is because I am quiet.
It enables me to think and feel at ease in such a chaotic world.
But who knows!
All I know is that poetry has helped me find myself *almost* fully.
And I say *almost*, because I'm not sure
we ever stop finding ourselves in one way or another.
Together with my writing,
my passion for music,
art, wildlife, and poetry in general,
I am more able to understand, and accept,
who I truly am.

Thank You
For Reading

Printed in Great Britain
by Amazon